# Jo's Big Paws

## SONICA ELLIS

# DEDICATION:

This book is dedicated to my beloved pet and best friend, Jo Lewis,
whose sweet nature, silly antics, unconditional love and never-ending affection
never failed to remind me that no matter what kind of day
I might have had, or how low I might have gotten,
someone had my back
...especially if I had treats :)

# ACKNOWLEDGMENTS

Thank you to all who helped me realize this dream of writing
my 1st children's book. My sincere gratitude to my illustrator, Harriet Rodis,
who did such a wonderful job of capturing the whimsical nature of our Jo.

Jo is an adorable little Boxer puppy with a bright tan coat and big brown eyes with black rings around them like a raccoon!

She has floppy brown ears that jiggle when she walks and a little stub for a tail that wiggles when she is happy.

But what Jo is most known for are her four

# big white paws!

Jo lives with her family - a loving
mom named Linda,
a dad named Anthony,
a Persian cat named Walter,
and Jo's favorite family member,
a beautiful 5-year-old girl named
Maddie.

Jo is a friendly puppy who loves to be helpful. On one particular morning Jo woke up feeling extra helpful.

"After breakfast I am going to help someone! I wonder who needs my help today!" thought Jo as she went into the kitchen to have her breakfast.

While she was eating her kibble, Jo noticed Walter the cat staring at her.

"Hmmmmm, Walter looks hungry. I bet he would like some of my breakfast" thought Jo, so she picked up her bowl in her mouth and began to walk over to offer some breakfast to Walter.

But before
she could take
three steps,
her paws got tangled up
and she stumbled,
spilling her kibble

# All over the kitchen floor!

Jo looked at the kibble spread out all over the floor. Jo looked at Walter and Walter looked back at Jo as if to say "You and your big paws did it this time! Mommy is going to be upset with you for spilling your breakfast."

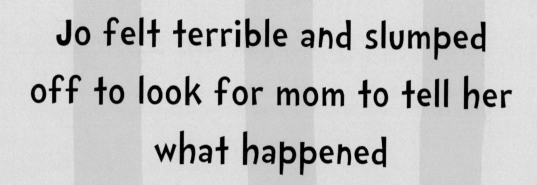

Jo felt terrible and slumped
off to look for mom to tell her
what happened

When Jo found Mom she had just finished folding the laundry and was getting ready to take it upstairs to put away.

Jo thought "Maybe if I help mom with the laundry she will not be upset that I spilled my breakfast!"

Jo was very excited by the idea and ran to help Mom, but before she could get 3 steps...

Jo stumbled

over

her

big

paws

again!

This time Jo did not spill anything, but she did stumble into Mommy's legs causing her to lose her balance and spill the laundry all over the floor!

"Jo, look at what you did! You and your big paws made me spill the laundry all over the floor!" exclaimed Mom.

Jo bowed her head and walked away sadly to look for Dad... "Maybe he needs my help" she thought. ---

Jo found Dad in the yard on top of a ladder painting the garage.

Jo thought to herself "That is a lot of painting to do. Maybe I can help Dad paint!"

Jo picked up a brush in her mouth and ran eagerly toward the ladder.

But what do you think happened? In her excitement she stumbled over her big paws and fell into the ladder causing Dad's paint can to fall from the ladder and spill all over the driveway!

"Jo! Look what those big paws have done! Now I have to clean up this mess! Go back in the house!"

Jo bowed her head once again, turned and slowly walked back into the house feeling terrible.

"My big paws are good for nothing" Jo was thinking as she walked down the hallway toward Maddie's room.
As she got nearer Jo heard Maddie crying!

Jo walked in and stood in front of Maddie as if to ask "Why are you crying Maddie?" Maddie said nothing.
Jo even wiggled her stub to see if that would get Maddie to stop crying, but that did not work.

So Jo sat down in front of Maddie and looked up at her. Maddie looked at Jo and said "Oh Jo, "Mom and Dad are too busy to play with me."

Upon hearing this Jo stood up, putting her big paws on Maddie's shoulders and nuzzled up against Maddie's neck.

"Oh Jo, you always make me feel better! You and your big paws give the best hugs!"

Jo's stub was wiggling!

Maddie was laughing and

Jo was happy!

She was finally able to help someone!

# THE END

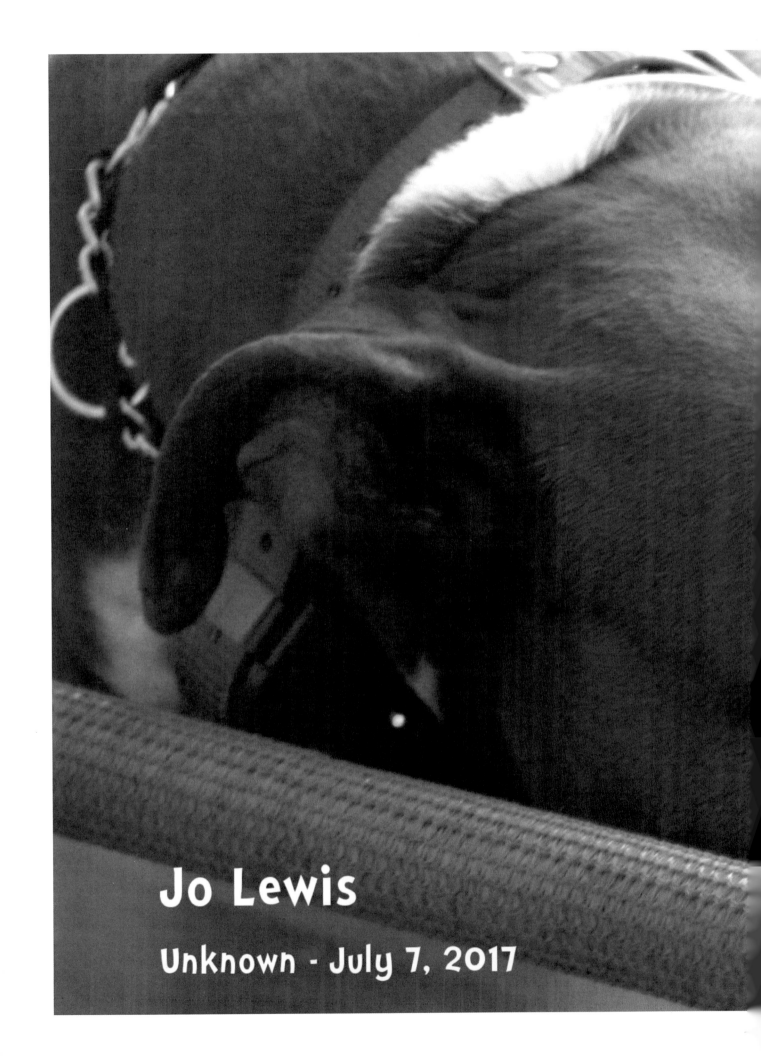

Jo Lewis

Unknown - July 7, 2017

Made in the USA
Las Vegas, NV
18 March 2022

45892580R00019